Stinky Pinky and the Hexaplex

Cynthia Turner

Print information available on the last page

Rev. date: 10/11/2017

To order additional copies of this book, contact:
Xlibris
1-888-795-4274
www.Xlibris.com
Orders@Xlibris.com

Stinky Pinky and the Hexaplex

Cynthia Turner

Reading is Fun !

Ms. Turner

It was a glorious day in Sunshine Bottoms. The sun peeked over the horizon and cast a beautiful shadow on the land. Stinky Pinky climbed out of his hay-covered bed and scanned his surroundings glad that this day had finally come. He was so excited about making the 100% Club at school that he could hardly contain his excitement.

3

Stinky Pinky and many other piglets in his class had worked real hard to make the 100% Spelling Club. Mrs. Sowsworth, their teacher had motivated the piglets to do their best and was very proud of their efforts.

5

This was the last test before the awards were to be given out and Stinky Pinky had not prepared himself. Mamma Pinky had been encouraging Stinky all week to study for his test. On Monday, she told Stinky to go to his room and study. Stinky had never disobeyed his mother before, but once out of sight, he pulled out his IPAD and started playing one of his favorite games; "Real Racing 3". Poor Stinky got caught up in his game and played for two hours.

On Wednesday, Stinky was supposed to study with his older brother, Slimy Pinky. When Slimy came to Stinky's room to help him study his words, Stinky acted like he was finished. Once Slimy left, Stinky pulled out his smart phone and started texting his friends.

When Thursday came, Stinky was supposed to take a trial spelling test with his middle brother, Scaly Pinky but instead went outside and played football with his neighbors.

Now today was Friday and Stinky had a plan. He knew that if he did not show up for school today he would automatically get into the 100% Club, so he decided to skip school and go down to the sea.

After breakfast, Stinky rushed to the door, kissed Mamma Pinky goodbye, and dashed towards the school like a freight train. But instead of making a right turn at the corner of Riblet Lane, Stinky turned left on Snout Parkway and headed down towards the sea. He could feel the cool, moist breeze as he rushed along.

Stinky strolled along the sea shore kicking a florescent rock as he dallied along. "Oh, oh ouch!" he heard someone say. Stinky looked down at his feet and discovered a blue sea creature staring up at him with wide, quizzical eyes.

"Hey, watch where you're going, be careful where you step"

"You're not light on your feet, you've got plenty of pep"

"I may be tiny and even slow"

"But if you're not careful, I'll bite off your toe"

Stinky stared in disbelief at the talking sea snail and said, "Who are you?"

"Why, I'm Harry Hexaplex and I live over there"

"With my mom, and dad, and my brother Ober"

"We are sea snails with special glands that secrete"

"A distinctive colored dye that is quite unique"

Stinky Pinky ogled the hexaplex with disbelief. He thought to himself, "secretion glands?" that's an unusual feature to have.

Stinky Pinky introduced himself to Harry then pondered for a moment as he watched the hexaplex turn five different colors. Then, in his most exciting voice, Stinky Pinky asked the hexaplex;

"Why are you changing colors, blinking red and green"

"You're the strangest sea creature that I've ever seen"

"Do you camouflage your body both night and day"

"Or hide from your mother when you turn grey"

Harry, the hexaplex grinned to himself knowing the secret that he was keeping from Stinky Pinky. You see, whenever the hexaplex told a lie, he would change colors and secrete a gaseous smell. He had been changing colors every fifteen minutes since he walked away from his house to go to Seaport Music School to take his music lessons. Harry's mother enrolled him in Mrs. Cee Urchin's class for his music lessons, but Harry decided that he wanted to have fun and frolic in the sea today. He started turning colors right when he rounded the corner just past his friend Jasper's house. Harry, the hexaplex knew that it was wrong to lie to his mother just like he knew that he shouldn't skip his music lessons.

"I was headed towards my music lesson today"

"But I don't want to go, I just want to play"

"My mom will never know just where I have been"

"For if she finds out, she'll surely keep me in"

SCHOOL OF MUSIC

But Stinky interrupted Harry and said with a frown;

"You're disobeying your Mother and lying to her"

"Hey that's not cool, he said with a slur"

"Why do you hurt her, make her feel ashamed"

"When you know that you are the one to blame"

The hexaplex lowered his head and breathed out a big sigh. He's right Harry thought. My mom taught us not to lie. I should go on and take my lesson and make Mamma real proud. I should do what is right and follow Mamma's directions.

23

The hexaplex turned to Stinky and said,

"Thanks Stinky Pinky you've told me what's right"

"I shouldn't lie, or steal, or start a big fight"

"I must honor my parents and be kind to my friends"

"I'll stay out of trouble for forgiveness of sins"

Stinky Pinky looked at Harry Hexaplex with a newfound respect. He realized that he was just as guilty as the hexaplex and that he should do the right thing, too. A solitary tear slid from the corner of Stinky's left eye.

With delayed excitement, he twirled around and reached out to grab Harry to thank him for reminding him to do what was right. Harry swirled around in the air with glee, oohing and aahing as he went.

Suddenly, Stinky Pinky dropped the hexaplex and shouted, "OOOOOOOOOOH! What is that smell?" Stinky didn't realize it, but he had accidently grabbed Harry's secretion gland and squeezed it until a foul smelling blue mist squirted out "That smell is savage!" choked Stinky. His hands began to burn, then turn blue. He carefully watched as his arms, his chest, his shoulders, and his ears began to turn blue, too.

"Oh no, cried the hexaplex, you're turning all blue"

"My dye changed your color right down to your shoe"

"How will you explain this, what will your mom say"

"When you go home and show her what happened today"

Stinky Pinky suddenly lowered his head in shame and began to weep. He was sure that his Mamma was going to be so disappointed in him. Not only did Stinky Pinky lie to his Mamma, he also deceived his family, friends, and teachers. This was indeed a **BLUE** day in his life.

The hexaplex felt like crying, too, but instead began to reassure Stinky Pinky.

"My new friend Stinky we've both done wrong"

"But I've learned my lesson now I can sing a new song"

"I've discovered that it's better to do what is right"

"Than to be a deceiver and loose trust overnight"

After a few minutes Harry told Stinky that he thought that it was time for him to go home. The two friends hugged and both agreed to go home and face the music. They went their separate ways thinking of the other as they slowly crept along.

When he made it to his front door, Stinky Pinky gazed through the window and saw his Mamma dusting the furniture. Gathering all of his strength Stinky turned the handle and cautiously pushed the door open.

"Mamma!" he called out. "I'm in trouble."

Startled by her son's voice at this hour, Mamma Pinky spun around and let out an alarming gasp when she saw Stinky. "Whu.............whu.............. what happened to you? Son, you are all blue!" "Yes Mamma, I turned blue. I have been naughty and I must tell you the truth."

Stinky sat down on the sofa and told his Mamma the whole truth. Mamma was so disappointed in her son but managed to listen without shedding any tears.

"Oh Stinky Pinky," said Mamma. "I think that you have punished yourself enough. You will be blue until the dye wears off. You will be laughed at by your friends. Your classmates, neighbors, and brothers will call you names and joke about your new image. My poor silly boy. Don't you know that it is better to obey your parents and to tell the truth than lie and face more consequences?"

"I know that now Mamma. I am very sorry for disobeying you," Stinky said sincerely.

"I've learned my lesson, I've learned it well"

"Will it benefit others, only time will tell"

"I hope my friends will speak only what is true"

"To avoid facing trouble and turning blue."

LESSON LEARNED

Obey your parents, do not lie, and for heaven's sake don't skip school!

CPSIA information can be obtained at www.ICGtesting.com
Printed in the USA
LVIW01n1334271017
553932LV00002B/3